Ellie and the Magic Computer

JEANETTE BEAUMONT

Illustrated by Janine Dawson

sundance Newbridge

The Story Characters

Ellie
is confused about magic.

Gary
likes computer games.

Shashi
has his own
pocket computer.

Mr. Bates
teaches the
computer class.

The Story Setting

TABLE OF CONTENTS

CHAPTER 1

Magic and Computers

Ellie knew about magic. She read stories about magic. In stories, things happen, and no one can explain why.

Gary never thought about magic, but he didn't read much. He was Ellie's brother. He was a little more than two years older than her.

Gary liked computers. When Ellie asked him, "Are computers magic?" Gary laughed.

"Computers only do what they are programmed to do," said Gary.

"What does programmed mean?" Ellie asked.

Gary tried to explain. "A computer is built by people to work things out. People write programs, and the computer does what the program says. Shashi and I are going to write some programs soon."

Gary and Shashi had met in computer
class. Shashi had his own pocket
computer.

Ellie was just about to start going to computer class, too. The worst part of the class was that it was going to be held during school vacation.

Everyone said how lucky they were.
They would learn how to use the
Internet and to play computer games.

But Ellie wasn't any good at computer games. She didn't really like them.

Ellie knew that her father wanted her to learn how to use computers.

"You will be able to find out about everything," he said. "It's magic what computers can do."

Ellie was confused about magic.

CHAPTER 2

Searching the Internet

Their teacher, Mr. Bates, was very nice. He wore glasses and a bow tie. He had a soft voice.

When he told the class to search the
Internet, he showed them how to get
started. But Ellie just sat there staring
at the screen.

"Look, Ellie!" called Gary. "Look what Shashi found on the Internet. It's a site all about elephants."

Gary knew Ellie liked elephants a lot.
Ellie wouldn't look. She wanted to find
things on her own. But she wasn't
very good at it.

Mr. Bates saw Ellie's sad face.

"Use this computer over here, Ellie,"
he said.

Mr. Bates pointed to a strange object in the corner of the room. It did not look like a computer. It looked more like a soccer ball.

"I'll let you get started, Ellie," said
Mr. Bates. Then he was gone.

"Where would you like to go today?"
asked a voice from the strange-looking
computer. Ellie was startled.

"What do you mean?" she cried.

CHAPTER 3

What Is This Computer?

"Make up your mind! Make up your mind! What's so hard to decide?" grumbled the voice from the computer.

Ellie felt that this was unfair. "I don't know what you mean. I don't know what you are, and I don't know where you came from."

"I'm the brainiest brain," said the
voice from the computer. "I mean what
I want to mean. I am what I want to
be. I go wherever I want to go."

"So you think you know everything," said Ellie.

"Yes," agreed the voice. "WHERE DO YOU WANT TO GO TODAY?"

"I want to ride on an elephant," said Ellie firmly.

"Alone, or with them?" asked the voice, making it clear that it meant Gary and Shashi.

"With them, of course." She wanted
her brother and Shashi with her.

Before she could blink, Ellie was high up on the back of an elephant. Gary and Shashi were there with her. So was Mr. Bates.

Mr. Bates had a large hat on his head.

"My grandfather's pith helmet," he said grandly. "This will come in handy."

CHAPTER 4

The Magic Ride

Mr. Bates was right about the need for a hat. The sun was very hot as the elephant ambled along.

They were at the head of a long chain
of elephants. Their elephant had a
wide seat on its back. Shashi said the
seat was called a *howdah*.

The elephants seemed to know where they were going. They made their way up a steep slope.

Shashi was born in India, and he knew all about elephants. Shashi moved up onto the elephant's head. "Look at the top of the hill," he called.

"Don't shout in my ear," grumbled the elephant. Gary and Shashi were startled.

"Sorry," they both said.

"Hey, this must be India," added Gary.

"Of course it is," said Shashi, "and this is an Indian elephant. You can tell by his ears."

"Her ears," said the elephant grumpily.
"I am taking you to the Amber
Palace."

When they reached the top of the hill, there it was. The Amber Palace was grander than anything Ellie had ever seen in books.

"Ambling to Amber, seated on a howdah," Mr. Bates said softly.

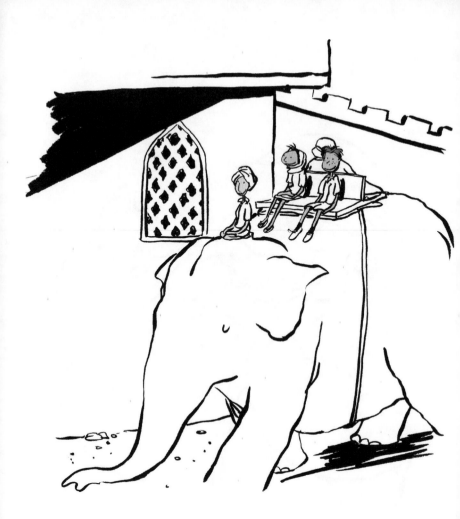

The elephants moved faster now. They seemed to be happy to leave the dusty road. They walked around the palace courtyard.

Ellie thought that the people who lived here must have been very grand, or splendid.

"Yes indeed, very splendid," said Mr. Bates. "What a life they had!"

"Ah yes," agreed the elephant. She
told them all about the time that the
prince had ridden on her back.

"It was a very special day. I had bells around my feet. My back was covered with a silver and gold cloth."

They stopped at a balcony. "Here is where the prince walked straight onto my back," said the elephant.

A man stepped onto the balcony. He put something into Ellie's hand. It was a photo of all of them on the elephant's back. Ellie put the photo into her pocket.

CHAPTER 5

Ellie Knows What Magic Is

The voice from Ellie's computer called, "You are out of time. All out of time!"

The elephant had just walked into a
garden. Instead of trees, the garden
had huge, stone pillars.

Suddenly, the stone garden became
the yard outside their classroom. The
elephant was gone.

Ellie was with Gary. The class was over. They were waiting to be picked up by their father.

"Hi, kids," said their father, as he pulled up in the car. "How did you do today?"

"We rode on an elephant," said Ellie. "You are right, Dad. Computers are magic."

Gary laughed. "We were on the Internet, Dad," he said.

Ellie felt confused again. Had she just
imagined the whole thing? Her eyes
got all watery.

If she closed her eyes, she could still feel the elephant move and sway. She could feel the heat of the sun.

She reached into her pocket for a tissue. She still had the photo!

There they all were on the elephant.
Mr. Bates wore his pith helmet. He
sat on the howdah with Gary and
Ellie. Shashi was up in front on the
elephant's head.

"Look, Gary," Ellie said, showing him the photo.

"COOL," said Gary. "You made this? Is that what Mr. Bates taught you? Wait until Shashi sees this. COOL!"

Ellie did not say any more. She knew there were some things you couldn't explain. She held the photo tightly. She knew about magic.

GLOSSARY

ambled
walked slowly

balcony
a platform high up on the
side of a building

howdah
an Indian word for
a seat on an elephant

pillars
tall posts or
columns

pith helmet
a hard hat worn in very hot places

site
a place to go on the Internet

steep
very high

sway
to rock from side to side

Talking with the Author and the Illustrator

Jeanette Beaumont (author)

Who is your favorite cartoon character?
Bugs Bunny.

Why is the sky blue?
To match the sea.

What are three things that you can't live without?
Family, friends, and books.

Janine Dawson (illustrator)

If you could go anywhere at all, where would it be?
I'd go to the moon.

Why is the sky blue?
Because it's soothing and refreshing and goes with all of the colors the world has to offer.

What are three things that you can't live without?
My daugher Rosie, colors, and a good laugh.

sundance Newbridge

Copyright © 2002 Sundance Newbridge Publishing

All rights reserved. No part of this publication may be reproduced, stored in a retrieval system or transmitted in any form or by any means, electronic, mechanical, photocopying, recording, or otherwise, without the prior written permission of the publisher.

Published by Sundance Newbridge Publishing
33 Boston Post Road West, Suite 440, Marlborough, MA 01752
800-343-8204
SundanceNewbridge.com

Copyright © text Jeanette Beaumont
Copyright © illustrations Janine Dawson

First published 1999 as Sparklers by
Blake Education, Locked Bag 2022, Glebe 2037, Australia
Exclusive United States Distribution: Sundance Newbridge Publishing

ISBN 978-0-7608-5138-8

Printed by The YGS Group
Manufactured in York, PA USA
January 2022
The YGS Group Job #: D133783
Sun/New PO#: 229704